This 1995 edition published by Derrydale Books,
distributed by Random House Value Publishing, Inc.,
40 Engelhard Avenue, Avenel, New Jersey 07001
© 1994 Jane Wardle and Georgina Hargeaves.
Produced by Emma Books Ltd., Beckington, Somerset, U.K.
Illustrated by Georgina Hargreaves. Printed in Italy.
A CIP Catalog Record for this book is available from the Library of Congress.
ISBN 0-517-12060-7

Random House
New York • Toronto • London • Sydney • Auckland

Prince Brownie - Champion

Written by Jane Wardle
Illustrated by Georgina Hargreaves

DERRYDALE BOOKS
NEW YORK • AVENEL

The stable yard was buzzing with activity. Children were struggling with heavy buckets, spilling water down their jodhpurs. Ponies were tied to every possible post having their tails washed, hooves oiled and sleek coats groomed.

The yard was scattered with wheelbarrows, haybales, buckets and brooms. Some children were giggling and chatting over stable doors while others were despairing over the state of their ponies. One pony had just managed to undo the rope on her bridle and to find a dusty spot in which to have a good roll.

Jane was standing on an overturned bucket, trying to reach Prince Brownie's neck in order to braid his mane. Although her mother was holding on to his bridle, the pony was hindering her by nodding his head up and down. Unfortunately, his mane was so thick that the braids looked like a row of footballs down his neck. "Well, that is the best that I can do," said Jane stepping off the bucket and looking at her handiwork.

Prince Brownie's beautiful bay coat shone from all the loving effort that had been put into grooming it. His braided mane showed off his thick muscular neck and his eyes shone with the excited knowledge that he would have a day out tomorrow. He was obviously aware of how wonderful he looked.

It was the Rowarth County show and nearly everyone at the farm was competing. Jane and Prince Brownie were entered into the Gambler's Stakes competition in the morning, and the Fancy Dress in the afternoon, with Jane's friends Karen and Debbie. Prince Brownie was now ready for the following day and Jane put him into the stable for the night and gave him his dinner.

There was still plenty of activity in the yard and the excited pony could not settle down. He bucked and thrust his head over the stable door to see what was going on, dropping food from his mouth. "Hey you," cried Jane's mother, "Stop spilling your dinner. Pony feed doesn't grow on trees, you know!"

Jane's mother went home and dusk began to fall. The yard became quiet and Prince Brownie soon began to feel bored. Very soon he started to look around his stable for something to do. By the time Jane arrived early the following morning, his stable was a mess.

"Look at the state of this stable!" cried Jane's mother. "He has knocked my radio off the window ledge and trampled it, his hayrack is missing, and to top it all off, he has rubbed out most of his braids." But in no time at all, Jane had rebraided his mane, found his hayrack and cleaned up his stable. Along with her friends, they set off for the show.

All the way there, Prince Brownie insisted on leading the way and tried to kick the other ponies when they got too close, but they arrived at the rapidly filling showground safe and sound. "Look at all the people here," Jane said to Karen as they entered through the gateway, which was already getting churned up by the tires of horsetrailers.

"Oh, I am nervous," replied Karen, "I think I 'll go and see if I can enter
for the Handy Pony competition and then I 'll meet you at the ringside."
Prince Brownie was in his element on the showground. He showed off
all the way to the ringside, arching his neck and side stepping all the way.

15

Jane's parents walked across the grass to meet them carrying
buckets, coats, bridles and plastic bags filled with all sorts of
things. "We have just been over to the judge's trailer and
there is a big box of candy for the winners of the
Gambler's stakes," said her father.

Jane told her pony, "If we win I will
share it with you."

It was not long until the start of their class. Jane explained the rules to her parents. "Each fence has a value of points," she said, "We have two minutes to jump as many fences as we can without knocking any down. I am going to jump all the fences with the highest values and see if we can get the most points."

Jane and Prince Brownie began to warm up in the waiting ring as they waited for their turn. As soon as they entered the arena, Jane could sense that Prince Brownie was in a mischievous mood.

When she asked him to canter he began to buck and buck. He bucked the whole way around the course, but still managed to clear every fence by at least a foot. When the last bell rang to indicate the end of two minutes, Jane left the ring exhausted.

"Considering Prince Brownie's unusual style," said her mother, "I am amazed to say you are actually leading with 180 points."

Jane hugged her pony and gave him a whole pack of candy before flopping on the grass to watch the remainder of the competitors. Her father battled to hold Prince Brownie's reins when the naughty pony decided that it would be nice to eat the grass under the blanket on which a lady was sitting.

"He's good," said Jane as a boy rode in on a pretty piebald pony, "He's called Anthony and his mother helps to run the show." Anthony came very close with 175 points. Jane and Prince Brownie won, but only received a ribbon when the prizes were handed out.

Jane turned to Anthony and said that she thought there was a box of candy for the winners of this class. He smugly replied, "There was, but I didn't want to win candy, so I asked my mother to make them the prize for the Handy Pony class."

Jane was shocked by his arrogance, and said to Brownie, "Well, we showed him, Brownie," and they all had hotdogs and icecream to make up for it.

"You're so funny," Jane said quietly to her pony, "You bite, you buck all the way around the course, you are always up to mischief and yet you always win." Jane was beginning to understand that even if you are not perfect you can still find success. Prince Brownie truly was a winner.